FOR MUM AND DAD, WITH LOVE

LCC Number: 94-76897
ISBN 0-307-17518-9

Printed in Hong Kong
A MCMXCV

First published in Great Britain in 1995 by Frances Lincoln Limited,
4 Torriano Mews, Torriano Avenue, London NW5 2RZ.

SHOUTING SHARON

A RIOTOUS COUNTING RHYME

DAVID PACE

ARTISTS & WRITERS GUILD BOOKS
Golden Books
Western Publishing Company, Inc.

1

One daring Desmond ready to dive
and Sharon shouted . . .

JUMP!

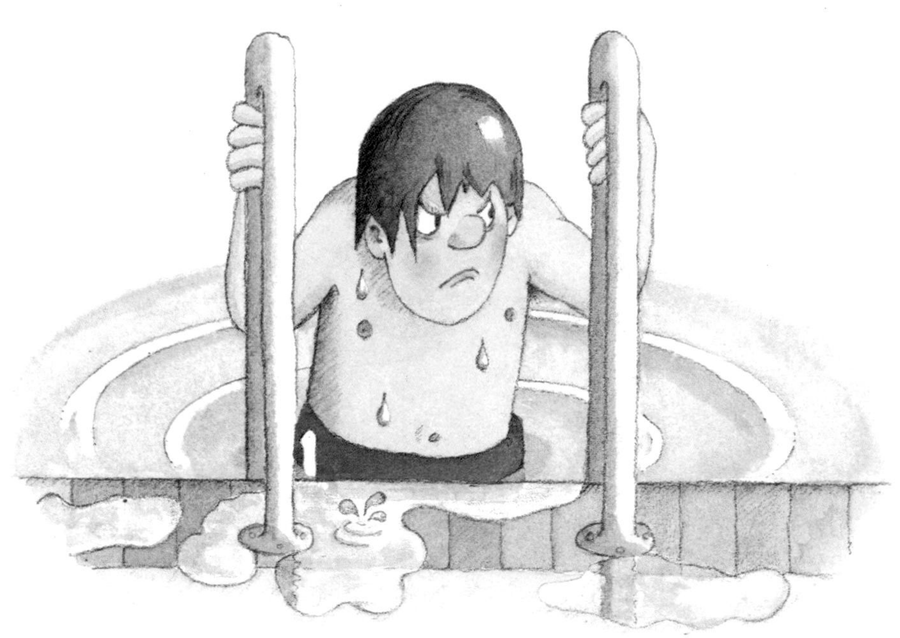

2

Two tired twins asleep in a carriage
and Sharon shouted . . .

WAKE UP!

3

Three busy barbers snipping beards
and Sharon shouted . . .

CUT!

4

Four fat ladies trying to lose weight
and Sharon shouted . . .

CHOCOLATE!

Five French chefs cooking food for a feast and Sharon shouted . . .

YUCK!

Six acrobats on a flying trapeze
and Sharon shouted . . .

CATCH!

7

Seven proud dogs posing for a picture
and Sharon shouted . . .

CATS!

8

Eight explorers entering a deep dark cave
and Sharon shouted . . .

BATS!

9

Nine musicians marching by
and Sharon shouted . . .

HALT!

Ten lions licking their lips

10

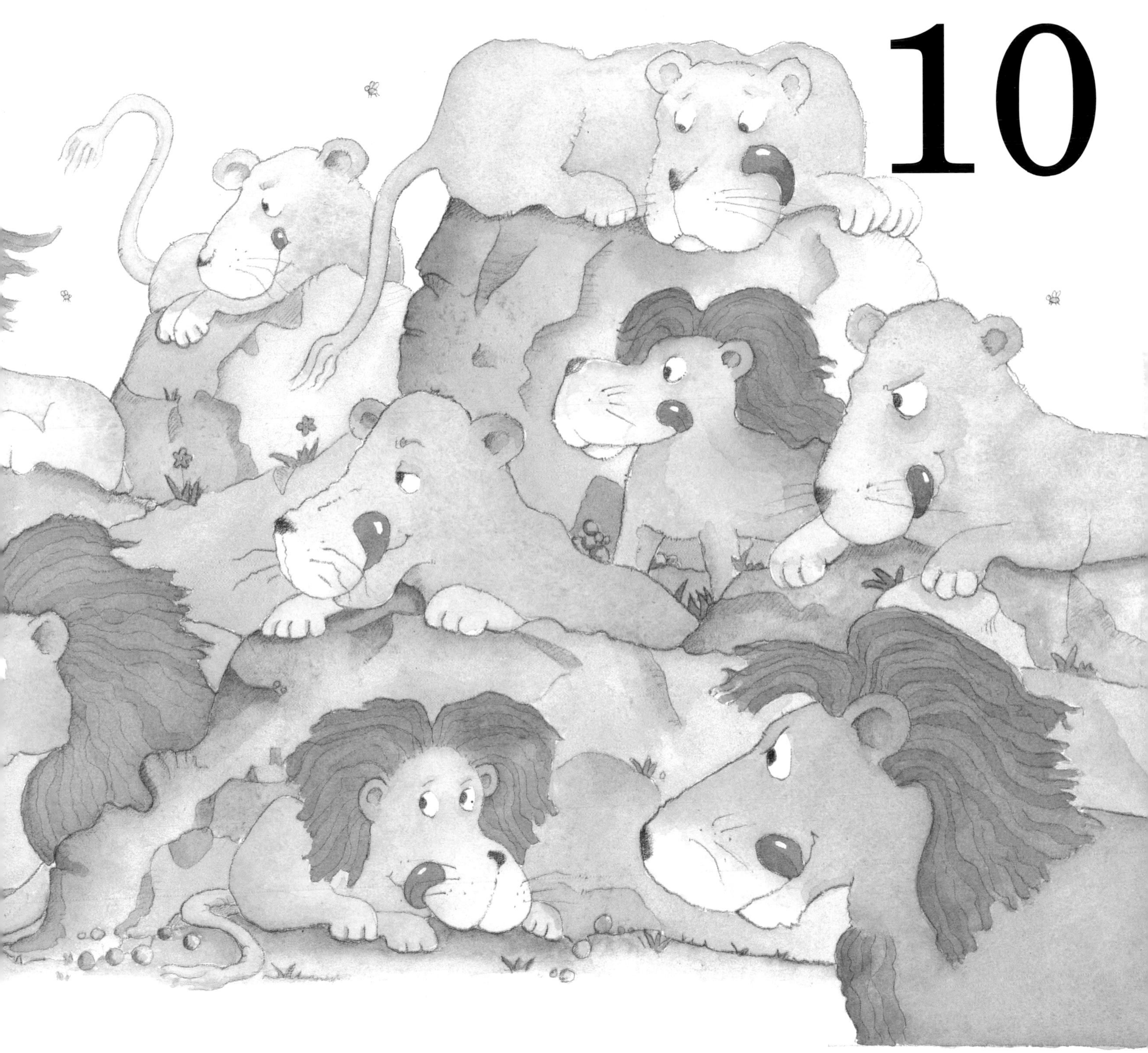

and Sharon shouted . . .

HE

LP

help...

But nobody came.

So Sharon shouted . . .

RRRRRRRR

And that was the end of that.